MARGRIT CRUICKSHANK grew up
in Scotland and read French and German at the University
of Aberdeen. She spent several colourful years
as a van-driver, waitress, postwoman and teacher before
beginning a career writing for children. Her previous
books for Frances Lincoln are *Down by the Pond* and *Don't Dawdle,
Dorothy!* Margrit lives in Dun Laoghaire, County Dublin.

ROSIE REEVE grew up in London
and attended Richmond College before moving on
to study Fine Art at Oxford University.
This is her first children's book. Rosie lives
with her family in West London.

*In memory of my mother, an inveterate duck-feeder ~ M.C.*
*For Jenny Reeve ~ R.R.*

First published in Great Britain in 2003 by
Frances Lincoln Children's Books, 4 Torriano Mews,
Torriano Avenue, London NW5 2RZ

www.franceslincoln.com

First paperback edition 2004

British Library Cataloguing in Publication Data
available on request

ISBN 1-84507-261-8
Set in Layout Regular

Printed in Singapore
9 8 7 6 5 4 3 2 1

# We're Going to Feed the Ducks

Margrit Cruickshank © Illustrated by Rosie Reeve

FRANCES LINCOLN

We're going to feed the ducks!

Look! What a friendly brown dog!

No! We're not going to feed
the friendly brown dog.
We're going to feed the ducks.

Look! **TWO** squirrels with bushy red tails!

No! We're not going to feed the squirrels
with bushy red tails.
We're going to feed the ducks.

Look! **Three** cheeky little sparrows!

No! We're not going to feed
the cheeky little sparrows.
We're going to feed the ducks!

Look! **Four** fat pigeons!
Listen to them go *prruuu, prruuu, prruuuuu!*

No! We're not going to feed
the fat noisy pigeons.
We're going to feed the ducks!

Look! **Five** squabbling seagulls!
Aren't they rude!

No! We're not going to feed
the rude squabbling seagulls.
We're going to feed the ducks!

Oh, all right then. We'll toss a few crusts
to the **five** squabbling seagulls.
There you are, seagulls!

We might as well give the
**four** fat pigeons some too.
There you are, pigeons!

And the **three** cheeky little sparrows.
I suppose we can spare them a few crumbs.
There you are, sparrows!

Do you think the **two** squirrels
will eat out of our hands?
There you are, squirrels!

The friendly brown dog's begging!
We'll have to let him have a slice as well.

Now we can feed the ducks!

Oh! Sorry ducks.
The bread's all gone!

All right. We'll get you some more.

We're going to feed the ducks!

### Don't Dawdle, Dorothy!

Margrit Cruickshank
Illustrated by Amanda Harvey

Trailing home behind her mother after a long morning's shopping,
Dorothy closes her eyes and when she opens them, the figure in front begins to change
shape: into a Snow Queen, then an ogre, then a grumpy old bear. But in the end
Dorothy's mother makes everything all right again.

ISBN 0-7112-1404-2

### Down By The Pond

Margrit Cruickshank
Illustrated by Dave Saunders

In this twist-in-the tail romping rhyme, a peaceful farmyard
erupts into a riotous hullabaloo. This is a book that will have children barking,
mooing and clucking along.

ISBN 0-7112-0978-2

### Out For The Count

Kathryn Cave
Illustrated by Chris Riddell

When Tom finds it hard to sleep, counting sheep
is just the beginning. Counting pythons and pirates, tigers, goats and ghosts
is much more fun. Written in lively verse, this counting adventure
goes all the way to one hundred.

ISBN 0-7112-0665-1